# CRUSADERS, AZTECS, SAMURAI

## From AD600 to AD1450



Dr Anne Millard

Illustrated by Joseph McEwan
Designed by Graham Round
Edited by Jenny Tyler and Robyn Gee

## Contents



Consultant Editors: Brian Adams, Verulameum Museum, St Albans, England; Professor Edmund Bosworth, Dept of Near Eastern Studies, University of Manchester, England; Ben Burt, Museum of Mankind, London, England; George Hart, British Museum, London, England; Dr Michael Loewe and Dr C. D. Sheldon, Faculty of Oriental Studies, University of Cambridge. England.
First published in 1978 by Usborne Publishing Ltd, Usborne House, 83-85 Saffron Hill, London EC1N 8RT.

Printed in Belgium.

# The Beginning of a New Religion

Soon after AD600,* in the land of Arabia, a man called Muhammad was preaching a new religion. He believed in Allah, the "One God". By the time of his death, most people in Arabia followed his religion and called him the Prophet.

In Europe, most people in the Roman Empire were Christians. But when the Empire was invaded, many of them began worshipping other gods. The eastern part of the Roman Empire (called the Byzantine Empire) was not invaded and stayed Christian.

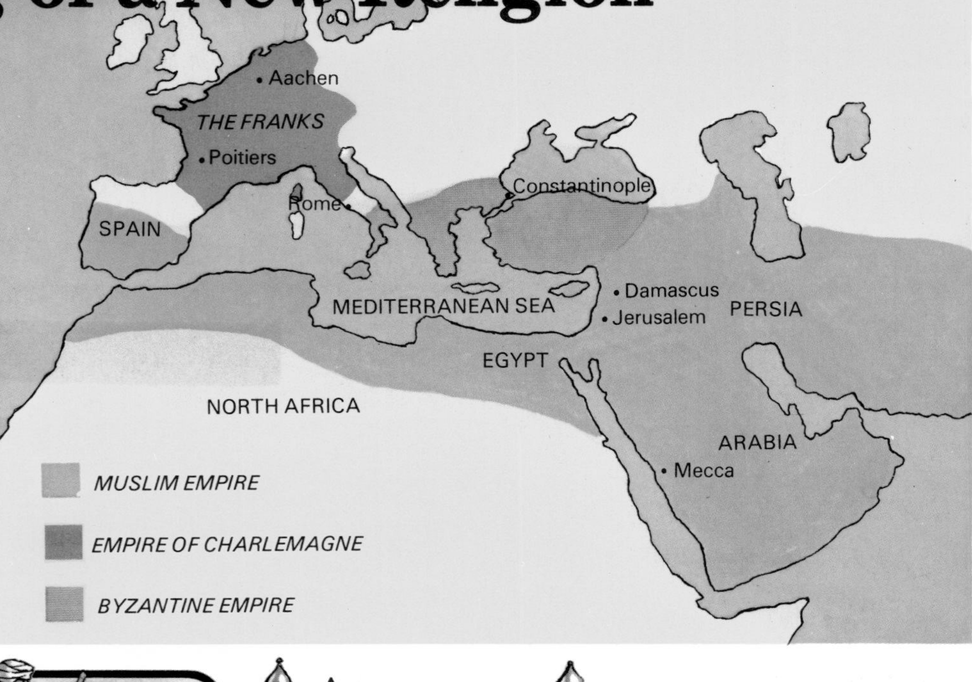

The teachings of Muhammad were collected and written down in a book called the Koran. His faith became known as Islam and his followers were called Muslims.

The caliphs, who were Muhammad's successors, believed that everyone should become Muslims. They fought many wars to spread their faith and conquered a great empire.

These Muslims are making a pilgrimage to Mecca, the home of Muhammad. All Muslims are meant to visit Mecca at least once in their lives.

Muslims eat and drink only at night during the month they call Ramadan. Good Muslims also give money to the poor.

Muslims should pray five times every day, facing towards Mecca. On Fridays, prayers are said in buildings, like this, called mosques.

* *AD stands for two Latin words. Dates with AD next to them are that number of years after the birth of Christ.*

# Christians in Europe

The Christian Church in western Europe was led by the Pope, seen here with one of his priests. Many popes sent out missionaries to persuade people to become Christians.

Some missionaries were killed by the people they tried to convert. It was several hundred years before people in Europe accepted Christianity as their religion.

The Muslims began to invade southern Europe. In AD732, Charles Martel, king of a people called the Franks, stopped their advance by defeating them at the Battle of Poitiers.

This is Roderigo of Bivar, who was known as El Cid, which means "The Lord". He helped to keep the Muslims out of northern Spain and became a great Christian hero.

In AD768, Charlemagne (Charles the Great) became King of the Franks. He conquered a lot of Europe and became its first great leader since the fall of the Roman Empire.

Charlemagne forced the people he conquered to become Christians, and fought the Muslims in Spain. On Christmas Day AD800, Pope Leo III crowned him Holy Roman Emperor.

7

This gold image of Charlemagne was made to put his skull in.

After Charlemagne's death his empire was divided. The Holy Roman Emperors ruled only the German-speaking peoples of Europe from then on, but were still very powerful.

Emperors and popes often quarrelled over power. After one quarrel, Pope Gregory VII kept Henry IV waiting in the snow outside Canossa Castle for three days before he would forgive him. Quarrels between other emperors and popes resulted in long, bitter wars in Germany and Italy.

## Key dates

| | |
|---|---|
| AD570/632 | Life of **Muhammad.** |
| AD622 | First year of the Muslim calendar. |
| AD630 | Mecca surrendered to Muhammad. |
| AD635 | Muslims captured Damascus. |
| AD637/642 | Muslims conquered Persia. |
| AD638 | Muslims captured Jerusalem. |
| AD641/642 | Muslims conquered Egypt. |
| By AD700 | All North Africa conquered by Muslims. |
| AD732 | Battle of Poitiers. |
| AD768/814 | Reign of **Charlemagne.** |
| AD800 | **Charlemagne** crowned Holy Roman Emperor. |
| AD1077 | Meeting at Canossa between **Henry IV** and **Gregory VII.** |
| AD1043/1099 | Life of **El Cid.** |

# Life in Viking Times

In Denmark, Norway and Sweden there lived a people called the North or Norsemen. They were farmers, fishermen and traders. Norsemen who sailed abroad were called Vikings. Some Vikings settled in France and became known as Normans.

Vikings lived in settlements like this one. The wall and part of the roof of the chief's house have been cut away so that you can see inside.

The Vikings were skilled wood-carvers and metal-workers. This carved wooden head is from a wagon.

Memorial stones to the dead were sometimes set up. These usually had letters called runes carved on them.

This is the grave of a Viking warrior. Later it will be covered with earth. His possessions, including his animals and sometimes even a slave, were buried with him. The Vikings believed that dead warriors went to "Valhalla", the hall of the gods.

# Viking raiders

The Vikings were sailors, warriors and adventurers. At first they robbed and plundered other lands. Later they settled in many parts of Europe, including Iceland.

From Iceland they went to Greenland and from there they are thought to have reached America. Long poems, called sagas, were written about brave Viking heroes.

The Vikings in France (Normans) were great soldiers. In AD1066, William, Duke of Normandy conquered England. Another group set out and conquered Sicily and part of Italy.

## Where the Vikings went

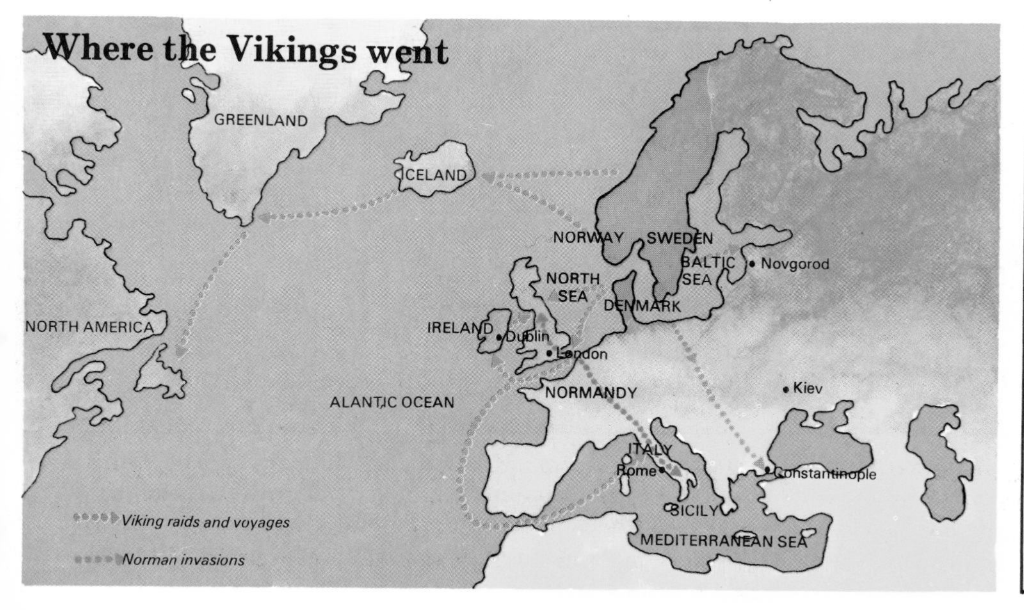


## Key dates

| | |
|---|---|
| AD793/900 | Great Viking raids on British Isles and northern France. |
| AD862 | Viking settlers in Kiev and Novgorod in Russia. |
| AD870/930 | Iceland colonized by Vikings. |
| AD900/911 | Normandy settled by Vikings. |
| AD960 | **Harald Bluetooth,** King of Denmark, converted to Christianity. |
| AD1000 | Vikings reached America. |
| AD1016 | **Knut** became King of England. |
| AD1066 | **William of Normandy** (William the Conqueror), descendant of Viking settlers, conquered England. Other Normans conquered part of Italy. |

# Kings, Knights and Castles

All the countries of Europe were organized in roughly the same way in the Middle Ages. A king or emperor ruled a whole country and owned all the land.

The king sometimes needed support or money for a particular plan. So he called a meeting of his nobles, bishops and specially chosen knights and townsmen to discuss it with him. This was the beginning of parliaments.

The king divided his land amongst his most important men. In return, they did "homage" to him. This meant that they knelt in front of him and promised to serve him and fight for him, whenever they were needed. These men were the nobles.

Each noble divided his land among knights who did homage to him. Peasants served a noble or knight and, in return, were allowed to live on his land. This arrangement of exchanging land for services is called the "feudal system".

Castles were uncomfortable places to live. They were damp, cold and draughty. Early castles had no glass in the windows and there was no running water. They were lit by torches made of twigs or rushes.

Kings and nobles built castles to protect themselves against enemies. These might be foreign invaders, other nobles or even rebellious peasants. We have taken away two walls so you can see inside.

## Becoming a knight

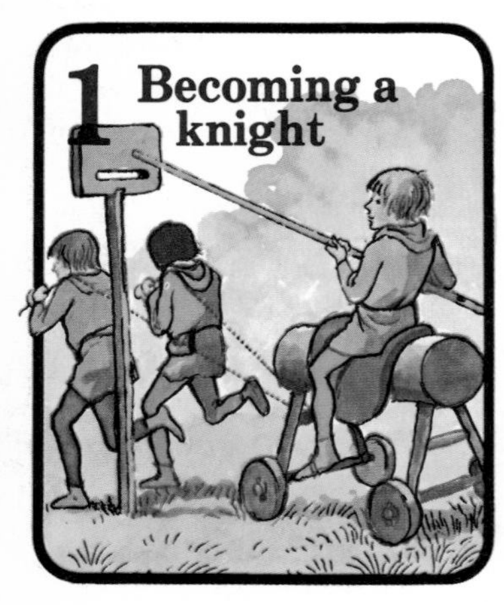


A boy who wanted to be a knight was sent to a noble's house as a page. He was taught to fight and to behave properly.

When he was older he became a squire. It was his job to serve a knight and to follow him into battle. Here is a squire with his knight.

If he proved himself to be worthy of the honour, a noble, perhaps even the king, would "knight" the young man.

The new knight's father or another noble usually gave him some land with peasants and villages. This was called a manor.

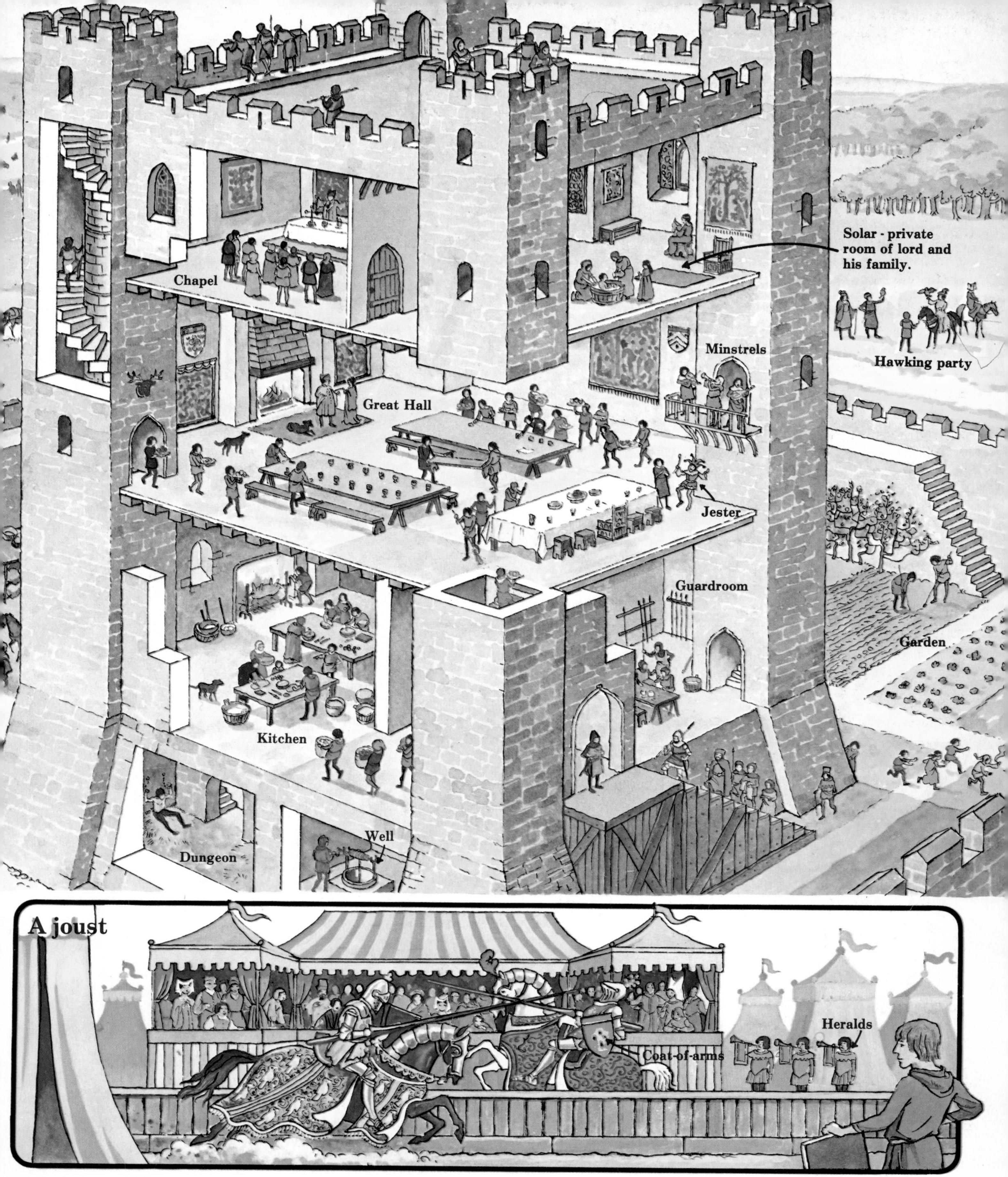


To keep in practice for battle, knights took part in specially organized fights. These were called tournaments or jousts. At a joust, two knights on horseback charged at each other with long lances, and tried to knock each other to the ground. Each noble family had a "coat-of-arms", which was painted on their shields, so they could be recognized in armour.

A knight wore a ribbon, badge or scarf belonging to his favourite lady. This was called her "favour". If he won he brought great honour to her as well as to himself.

# Village Life

In the Middle Ages, most people in Europe lived in villages. Each village was controlled by the Lord of the Manor. It usually had three fields, divided into strips, which the lord allowed the villagers to farm. They paid him by working for him and by giving him some of the food they grew.

All the peasants can use the common. They can graze their animals here and gather wood and berries.

Fisherman. The Church said people should always eat fish on Fridays.

The ford is a shallow part of the stream, where people can cross.

Ford

The villagers are holding a fair. This is their only chance to buy goods from outside the village. Jugglers, acrobats and musicians have come to perform at the fair.

Priest's house

Dancing bear

Merchants are coming to the fair to buy the villagers' wool.

Villagers harvesting wheat. Next year they will grow barley here.

## Black death

In AD1348, a ship from the East arrived in an Italian port. Some sick sailors came ashore bringing with them a terrible disease, known as the Plague or Black Death.

The Plague quickly spread across Europe because people knew little about medicine or the need to be clean. About one person in every three died from it.

Everyone has their grain ground into flour at the village mill.
The Lord of the Manor lives here in the Manor House.
Stray animals are put in a "pound" and their owners have to pay a fine before they can get them out.
In this field barley is growing. Next year it will be left unplanted.
Lord of the Manor going hunting. The peasants are forbidden to kill any game animals because that would spoil the lord's hunting.
Hole for smoke to come out.
Ale house
Blacksmith
Stocks
Roof made of straw or reeds. This is called thatch.
This field has been left fallow (unplanted) this year. This will make it more fertile for wheat next year.
Vegetable plot and garden.
Spinning wool
Tinker coming to fair to mend and sell metal pots and pans.

# Towns and Trade

This is what towns looked like in the Middle Ages. The streets were made of earth or cobbles and were narrow and dirty. There were no underground drains so people threw their rubbish into the street. Rich merchants built their houses of stone but most houses were made of wood, so fire was always a great danger. Towns were very small by modern standards and were surrounded by high stone walls.

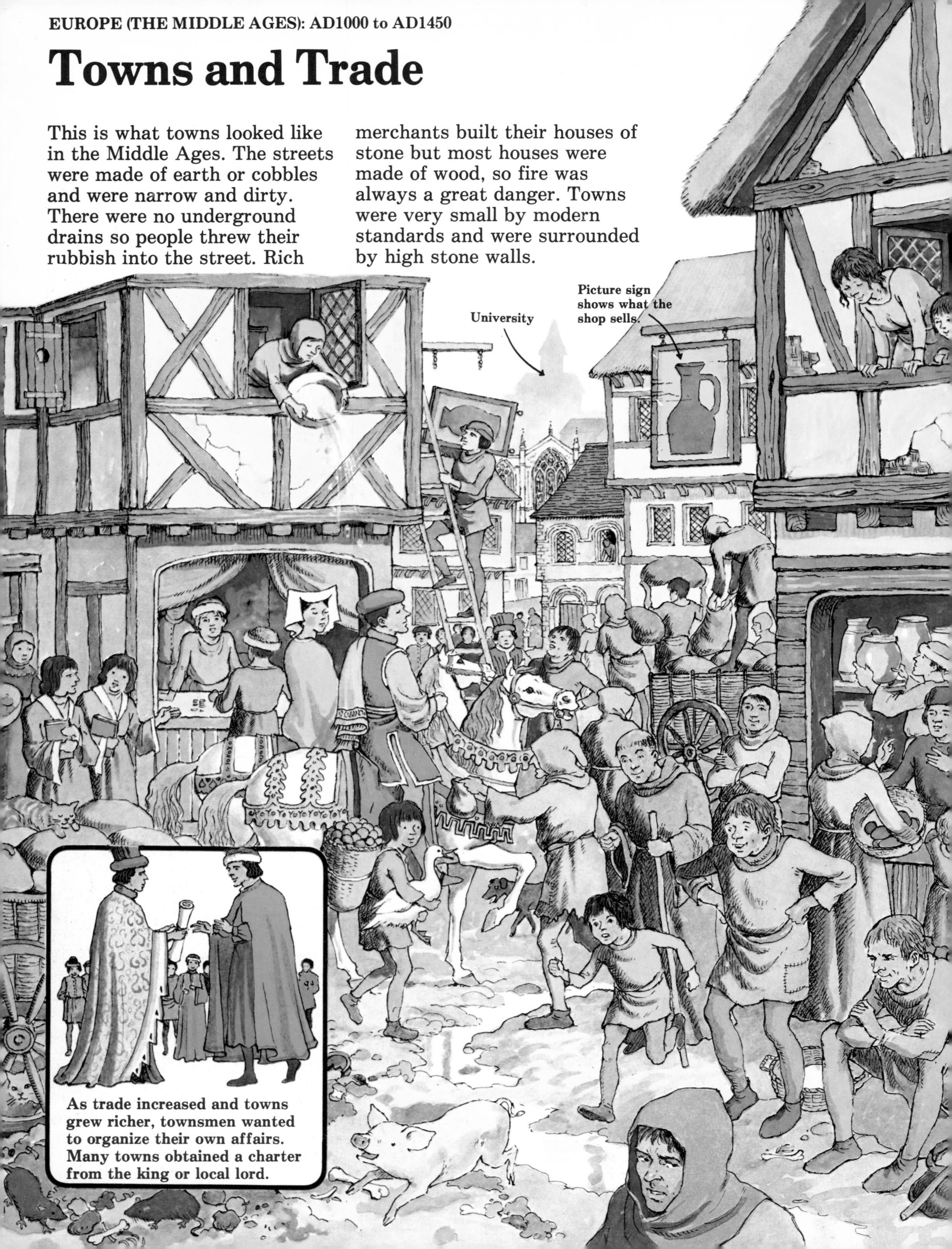


As trade increased and towns grew richer, townsmen wanted to organize their own affairs. Many towns obtained a charter from the king or local lord.

Each trade and craft had its own guild. The guild organized its members by fixing prices and standards of workmanship.

A boy who wanted to learn a trade was "apprenticed" to a master. He lived in his master's house and worked in his shop.

After seven years he made a special piece of work called a masterpiece. If it was good enough he could join the guild.

The mayor and corporation, who ran the city, were chosen from the most important members of each of the guilds.

When the population increased men could not find places as guild members so they had to work for others for wages.

On special holidays each guild acted different scenes from the Bible. These were called "mystery" plays. The guilds acted their plays

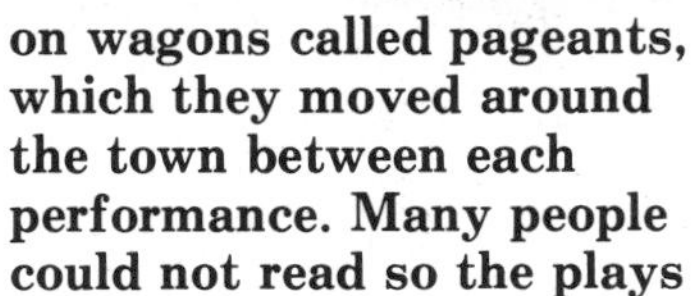

on wagons called pageants, which they moved around the town between each performance. Many people could not read so the plays helped them to get to know the stories in the Bible. In many towns the guild which did the best play won a prize.

The first bankers were rich merchants who lent money to people wanting to organize trading expeditions.

Spices, jewels and silks were brought to Europe from India and China. Italian merchants controlled this trade.

Goods were carried overland by packhorses. Most roads were very bad and there were often bandits in lonely areas.

Sea travel was also difficult and dangerous. Sailors steered by the stars and tried to keep close to the land whenever they could.

# The Church

The head of the Church in western Europe, the Pope, was elected by cardinals (the highest rank of priests) at a meeting called a conclave.

At one time there were three rival popes who all claimed to have been elected by a conclave. This argument was called the Great Schism.

Everyone went to church. All the services were in Latin, although only the priests and highly-educated people understood it.

Few people could read and write, except priests, so kings used priests as secretaries and advisers. Priests of high rank were summoned to parliament.

No one in Europe had discovered how to print books. All books were written by hand by monks and were often decorated with bright colours and gold leaf.

People who refused to believe everything that the Church taught were called heretics and were sometimes burnt to death. Joan of Arc was burnt as a heretic but later people decided she was a saint.

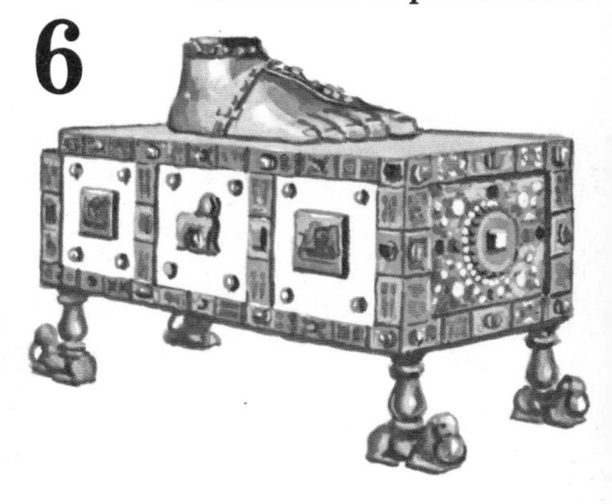


Bodies of saints or holy objects were often put into jewelled containers called reliquaries. These were treated with great respect and people worshipped in front of them.

## Pilgrims

Some people went on journeys to holy places to show their devotion to God, to be forgiven for some sin or cured of an illness. These journeys were called pilgrimages.

# Life in a nunnery

**Some people chose to give their lives completely to God's service and to live apart from the rest of the world. Women who did this were called nuns and lived in nunneries. Men were called monks and lived in monasteries. Trainee monks and nuns were called novices.**

**Nuns and monks promised to obey their superiors, to give up everything they owned and never to marry. Each day was divided into special times for prayer, study and work.**

**Like any Lord of the Manor, a nunnery had land. Rich people often left land and money to the nuns when they died, so that the nuns would pray for them. Some nunneries became extremely rich.**

## Key dates

| | |
|---|---|
| AD1181/1226 | Life of **St Francis of Assisi.** |
| AD1100s and 1200s | Quarrels between popes and emperors led to wars in Germany and Italy. |
| AD1265/1321 | The poet **Dante** lived. |
| AD1273 | **Rudolf of Habsburg** became King of the Germans. His family ruled until 1918. |
| AD1307/1314 | The Knights Templar were disbanded. |
| AD1337/1453 | The **"Hundred Years" War** between England and France. |
| AD1370/1417 | The Great Schism. |
| AD1380/1422 | Quarrels between French nobles helped the English in the war. |
| AD1412/1431 | Life of **Joan of Arc.** She led the French to victory in the war but was then burnt as a heretic. |

# Wars Between Religions

When invaders overran the western part of the Roman Empire, the eastern (Byzantine) half survived. The city of Constantinople was its capital.

These are priests of the Byzantine "Orthodox" Church. Over the years, eastern Christians developed slightly different beliefs from those of the west.

Between AD632 and 645 Muslims conquered part of the Byzantine Empire. Here their caliph (ruler) enters Jerusalem. Later, emperors and caliphs made peace.

Many Christian pilgrims visited the Holy Land, where Jesus had lived. The Muslims allowed them to continue these visits.

In AD1095, Pope Urban II gave a sermon at Clermont in France. He inspired his listeners to go on a crusade (holy war).

The Crusaders set out on the long and difficult journey to the Holy Land to win it back from the Muslims.

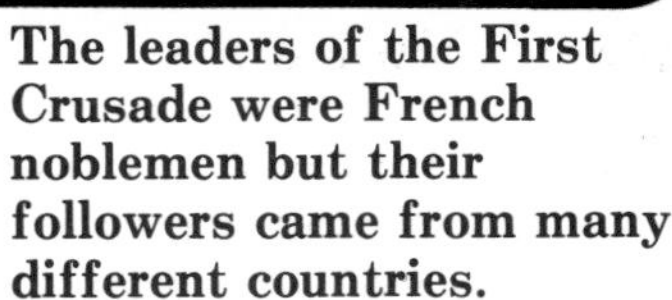

The leaders of the First Crusade were French noblemen but their followers came from many different countries.

The Crusaders arrived in Constantinople and met the Emperor. At first he was friendly but really he did not trust them.

The Muslims, under a great leader called Saladin, won back Jerusalem from the quarrelling Christians. Several new crusades set out from Europe to try to win it back.

The feeling between the Byzantines and the European Crusaders became so bad that one group of Crusaders attacked Constantinople itself and set up their own emperor.

Richard the Lionheart of England, Frederick II of Germany and St Louis of France tried to save Outremer but by AD1291 the Muslims had recaptured the Holy Land.

In the 11th century*, Seljuk Turks, who were also Muslims, arrived in the area from the east. They were very unfriendly to the Christians.

When the Turks defeated the Byzantines at the Battle of Manzikert, the western Christians felt they must go and fight to protect the Holy Land.

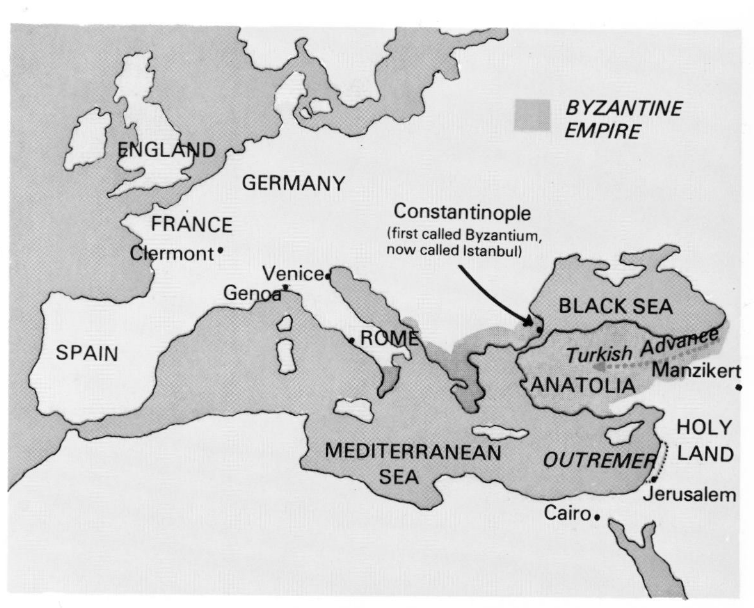


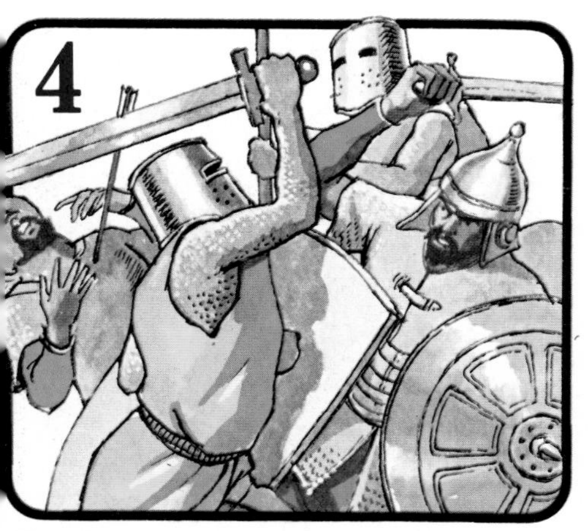


The Crusaders left Constantinople and went to fight the Muslims. They were very successful. The Holy Land became a Christian kingdom, called Outremer.

Special groups of soldier-monks were formed to care for pilgrims and to fight the Muslims. One knight from each of the three most important groups is shown here.

Some Crusaders settled in Outremer. When new Crusaders came out they were shocked to find the settlers quarrelling with each other but making friends with Muslim rulers.

The Byzantines won back Constantinople but the days of their wealth and power were over. In AD1453, with the help of cannons, the Turks finally captured the city.

## How to spot a Crusader's tomb

Here is the tomb of a knight. His crossed legs show that he was a Crusader. Look out for a tomb like this if you go inside a church.

## Key dates

| | |
|---|---|
| AD632/645 | Muslims seized parts of Byzantine Empire. |
| AD638 | Caliph Omar took Jerusalem. |
| AD1000/1100 | Turks invaded Byzantine Empire. |
| AD1071 | Battle of Manzikert. |
| AD1095 | Sermon at Clermont. |
| AD1096 | First Crusade. Jerusalem taken. Outremer founded. |
| AD1187 | **Saladin** took Jerusalem. |
| AD1191 | Crusade of **Richard the Lionheart.** |
| AD1204 | Sack of Constantinople. |
| AD1228/1244 | **Emperor Frederick II** won back Jerusalem for a while. |
| AD1249/1270 | Crusades of **St Louis** |
| AD1261 | Byzantine Emperor recaptured Constantinople. |
| AD1291 | The end of Outremer. |
| AD1453 | Turks captured Constantinople. (End of Byzantine Empire.) |

*This means the 100 years between AD1000 and AD1100.*

# How Muslim People Lived

The Arabs were the first Muslims and they conquered a huge empire. At first the whole Muslim empire was ruled by one caliph, but later it split into several kingdoms. Life for the Muslims was often more advanced than life in Europe. After they had conquered the eastern provinces of the Roman Empire, they absorbed many of the ideas of ancient Greece and Rome. Trading made them wealthy, and this brought more comfort and luxury into their lives.

**Many Arabs were nomads, who moved with their animals in search of water and pasture. They did not change their way of life even after they conquered their huge empire.**

**Peasants in Muslim lands went on working their fields. Much of the land was hot and dry and they had to work hard to keep it watered.**

**Houses in Muslim cities were often covered with white plaster, which helped to keep them cool. They faced inwards on to open courtyards, which provided shade. The streets were usually narrow and there were few open spaces except around the mosques.**

**Towns usually had a souq (market). The streets where it was held were often roofed over. Shops in one street usually sold the same kind of goods.**

**Palaces and many private houses had baths and there were also public baths. They were copied from the designs of Roman baths.**

**The Muslims developed a way of writing which read from right to left. Their system of numbers was simpler than the Roman figures used in Europe.**

**Muslim scholars studied Greek and Roman learning. They were especially interested in mathematics, the stars, geography, law, religion and medicine.**

**The Arabs made complicated instruments, like this one, which measured the position of ships at sea, by looking at the stars. This instrument is called an astrolabe.**

**Muslim doctors followed ancient Greek methods of treating the sick. Hospitals were built to care for people who needed special treatment.**

Muslim rulers built themselves huge palaces, like this one. These were beautifully decorated by skilled craftsmen, and were very comfortable, compared with European castles built at this time. They usually had gardens set out in patterns around fountains. Life in these palaces was very formal, with lots of ceremonies.

Part of a house was set aside for women only. This was called the harem. No man from outside the family could enter it. In the street, Muslim women wore veils.

## Arab traders

Trading played an important part in Muslim life. Arabs travelled to many different countries to find new customers. By sea they travelled in fast ships, called dhows. Some Arabs still use dhows today.

On land, merchants travelled by camel in groups called caravans. On main routes, caravansarays (shelters) were built at a day's journey from each other. Travellers could spend the night there.

## Muslim art

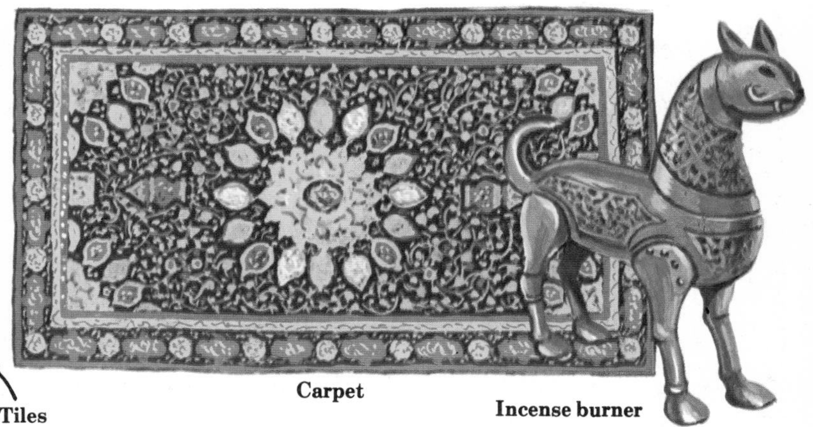


Their religion did not allow Muslim artists to make sculptures of the human figure. They used patterns, flowers, animals and birds as decoration. Tiles were often used for decorating buildings.

Muslim craftsmen were famous for the manufacture of beautiful carpets and for their metal work. The bronze lion, shown above, was used for holding burning incense. Crusaders who returned to the west took treasures like these back with them. The work of Muslim craftsmen became popular in Europe.

# Genghis Khan and his Empire

The Mongols were nomads who wandered across the plains of Asia with their herds of horses. From AD1206, a chief called Temujin overpowered all the Mongol tribes and conquered a huge empire. He became known as Ghengis Khan, the Great Prince. His sons raided Europe and his grandson, Kubilai Khan, conquered China. The Mongols were then weakened by family quarrels and fierce resistance. Later, a chief called Tamerlane* conquered an empire of his own and invaded India.

Muslim city being destroyed by Mongol raiders.

Mongols fought on horseback, using lances or bows and arrows.

Mongol commander. The Mongol army was very well-disciplined and could travel vast distances very quickly.

Here the Mongols are moving off after destroying an enemy city. The Mongols were very cruel to their enemies. Millions of people were killed or made slaves.

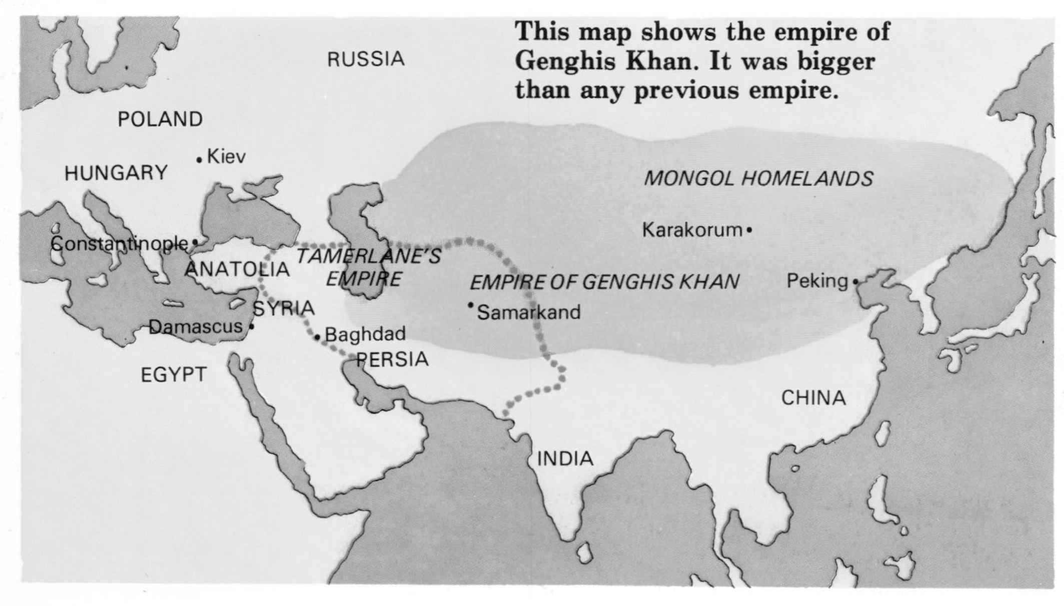


This map shows the empire of Genghis Khan. It was bigger than any previous empire.

## A friar visits the Mongols

A Christian friar, called William of Rubruck, was sent by St Louis of France to visit the Mongols. The Mongols had their own gods, but several of their

*Tamerlane is sometimes known as Tamburlaine.

## Key dates

| | |
|---|---|
| AD1206/1227 | **Genghis Khan** ruled. |
| AD1240/1241 | Mongols invaded Russia, Hungary and Poland. |
| AD1251/1259 | **Mongka** was Great Khan. |
| AD1253/1254 | Journey of **William of Rubruck.** |
| AD1258/1260 | Baghdad and Damascus sacked by Mongols. |
| AD1260 | Mongols defeated by the Egyptians. |
| AD1257/1294 | **Kubilai Khan** ruled in China. |
| AD1336/1405 | **Tamerlane** ruled. |
| AD1398 | **Tamerlane** invaded north India. |
| AD1402 | Mongols defeated the Turks. |

Genghis Khan organized his empire very efficiently. He drew up a clear law code called the Yasa, encouraged trade, punished bandits and started a messenger service.

Some Mongols settled in the newly conquered lands and built cities. Others continued to live as nomads in tents. There are Mongols who still live this way today.

princes had married Christian princesses. The Christians thought the Mongols would help them fight the Muslims, but this never happened.

This is the Mongol chief Timur the Lame, known in Europe as Tamerlane. He ruled his empire from the city of Samarkand.

This is the building in Samarkand where Tamerlane was buried. Russian archaeologists have opened his tomb.

By using modern methods scientists built up a face on his skull, so that we now know what he looked like.

# Princes and Temples

India was divided into kingdoms ruled by wealthy princes. They built themselves luxurious palaces and kept musicians and dancers to entertain them.

Indian villagers worked hard to keep their fields watered for growing rice. Each village was run by a headman who carried out the orders of the local ruler.

Indians did most of their trade with Arabs. They sold silks, ivory, pearls, spices and perfumes and bought Arab horses, which were especially beautiful and could run fast.

Many people, both inside and outside India, had accepted the teachings of the Buddha. Pilgrims, like this Chinese monk, travelled a long way to visit sacred Buddhist shrines.

5

The ancient Hindu faith became popular again. There were many gods and goddesses but the god Shiva, shown above, was one of the most important ones.

Hindus believe that all rivers come from the gods. The river Ganges, shown above, is especially holy. For thousands of years they have bathed in it to wash away their sins.

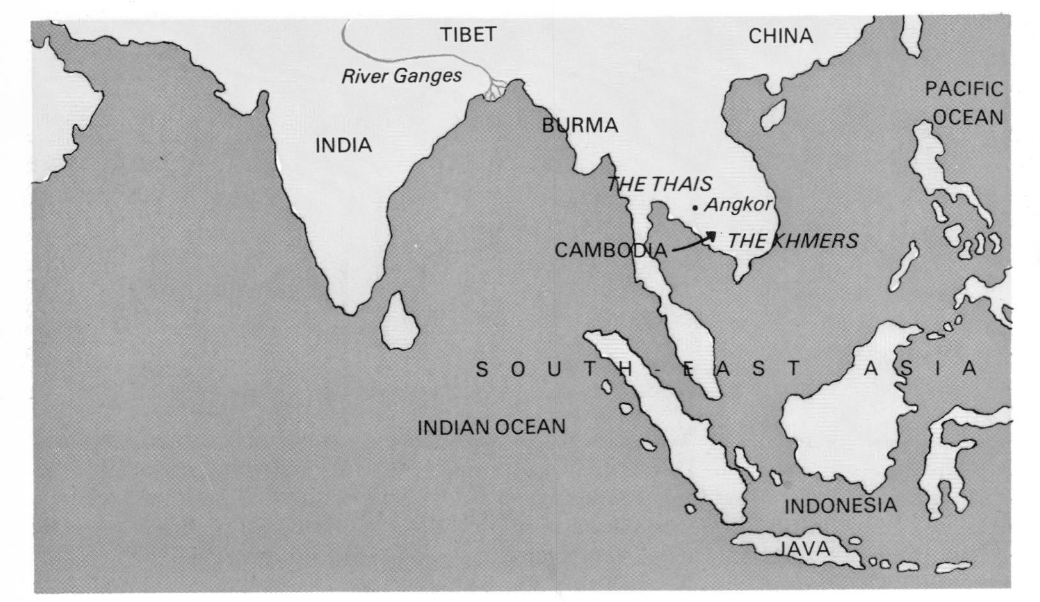


### Indian ideas in other countries

Indian religions, ideas and ways of life spread to other countries, especially in South-East Asia. This is a Buddhist temple at Borobudur on the island of Java in Indonesia.

# Angkor

## How we know

Pictures, like this, were cut into the stone of Angkor. They tell us about the battles, on land and rivers, fought by the Khmers against their enemies the Chams and Thais.

The stone carvings at Angkor also tell us about the everyday life of the Khmers. This picture shows two men and their friends getting ready to watch a fight between two cockerels.

One of the countries that was influenced by Indian ideas was Cambodia. In the ninth century a people called the Khmers rose to power there. They worshipped their own kings as gods on earth, but they also worshipped Hindu gods and built huge temples, like this one at Angkor. In AD1431 a people called the Thais invaded Cambodia. The great cities and temples of the Khmers were abandoned and the jungle grew up and covered them.

In AD1296 a Chinese visitor to Cambodia saw a procession like this and wrote an account of it.

# Silk and Spice Traders

In AD589 a new dynasty (family line) of emperors, called the Sui, began to rule China. They brought peace to the country after a time of long and difficult wars between rival Chinese groups.

Civil servants helped the Emperor to rule. They had to take exams before they were given jobs in government. In the countryside, the nobles, who owned most of the land, gradually became more powerful.

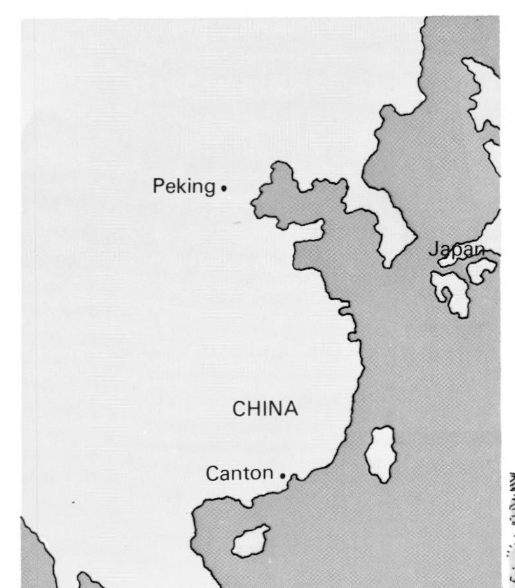

Buddhism had spread from India in the first century AD and was very popular. But many people still believed in the teachings of Confucius and the Taoist religion. At times Buddhists were persecuted.

## A trading city in China

Some merchants travelled by sea to Africa and the Middle East.

## Chinese inventions

The Chinese were the inventors of several things that were unknown to the rest of the world at this time.

They discovered how to make porcelain, a very hard, fine type of china.

At this time, the Chinese were using compasses to find their way across land and sea. This one is made of lacquered wood.

By the 10th century they were using wooden blocks to print books. This is probably the oldest printed page in the world.

Gunpowder was first used for fireworks. By the 13th century the Chinese were also using it for bombs and other weapons.

2

Chinese craftsmen were very skilful. At the time when the T'ang family were emperors (AD618/906) they made especially fine pottery figures of animals and servants. These were placed in tombs.

3

In AD1279 the Mongols, led by the great Kubilai Khan, overran China, which they then ruled for nearly 100 years.

## Key dates

| | |
|---|---|
| AD589/618 | Sui Dynasty ruled. |
| AD618/906 | T'ang Dynasty ruled. Buddhism very popular. |
| AD960/1279 | Sung Dynasty ruled. Growth of trade. Mongols started attacking northern frontier. |
| AD1279/1368 | Mongols ruled China. |
| AD1276/1292 | **Marco Polo's** trip to China. |
| AD1368 | Mongol rulers overthrown. |
| AD1368/1644 | Ming Dynasty ruled. |

Silk, porcelain (fine china) and carved jade were taken to the west and traded for silver and gold. Many cities grew rich because of this trade.

This caravan of camels is setting out with goods destined for the Middle East and Europe.

1 Marco Polo

Many foreign merchants, especially Arabs, came to China to trade. Later, a few adventurous Europeans arrived. Two of the European merchants who visited China were the brothers, Niccolo and Maffeo Polo, from Venice. On their second visit they took Maffeo's young son, Marco. Here they are meeting Kubilai Khan, the Mongol emperor of China.

2

Marco Polo travelled around Kubilai Khan's empire for nearly 17 years. When he returned home, he wrote a book about his travels. This is the first page of his book.

# Land of the Samurai

Japan is a group of islands off the coast of China. We know little about its early history because the Japanese had no writing until it was introduced from China in the fifth century AD. The Buddhist religion also came from China and won many followers, although Japan's ancient religion, Shinto, was still popular. Japanese arts, crafts, laws, taxes and the organization of government were also based on Chinese ideas.

SEA OF JAPAN

JAPAN

• Heian (now Kyoto)

PACIFIC OCEAN

**This is part of the Imperial city, Heian, later called Kyoto. The emperor was at the centre of power, but noble clans (families) gradually took over and ruled for him. Many emperors retired to Buddhist monasteries. As "Cloistered Ex-Emperors", some re-established their power for a time.**

**Legally all the land in Japan was owned by the emperor. He allowed farmers, like these, to use it in return for taxes and services. Later, the nobles began to acquire their own private lands because the Emperor was not strong enough to stop them. Many battles were fought about the possession of land and nobles gave it to their supporters as rewards.**

**This is Yoritomo, military leader and the chief of the Minamoto clan. In AD1192 he began to use the title "Shogun". This became the name for the head of government and was passed from father to son.**

**Poetry was popular, especially among the people at court. People made trips to look at the cherry blossom and see the maple leaves turning red. This inspired them to recite and write poems. There were several famous women poets.**

**The Japanese liked novels. This is Murasaki Shikibu, a court lady, who wrote a famous novel called *The Tale of Genji.***

**Japanese warriors wore suits of armour made of tough leather strips. This is an armourer's shop where the suits were made.**

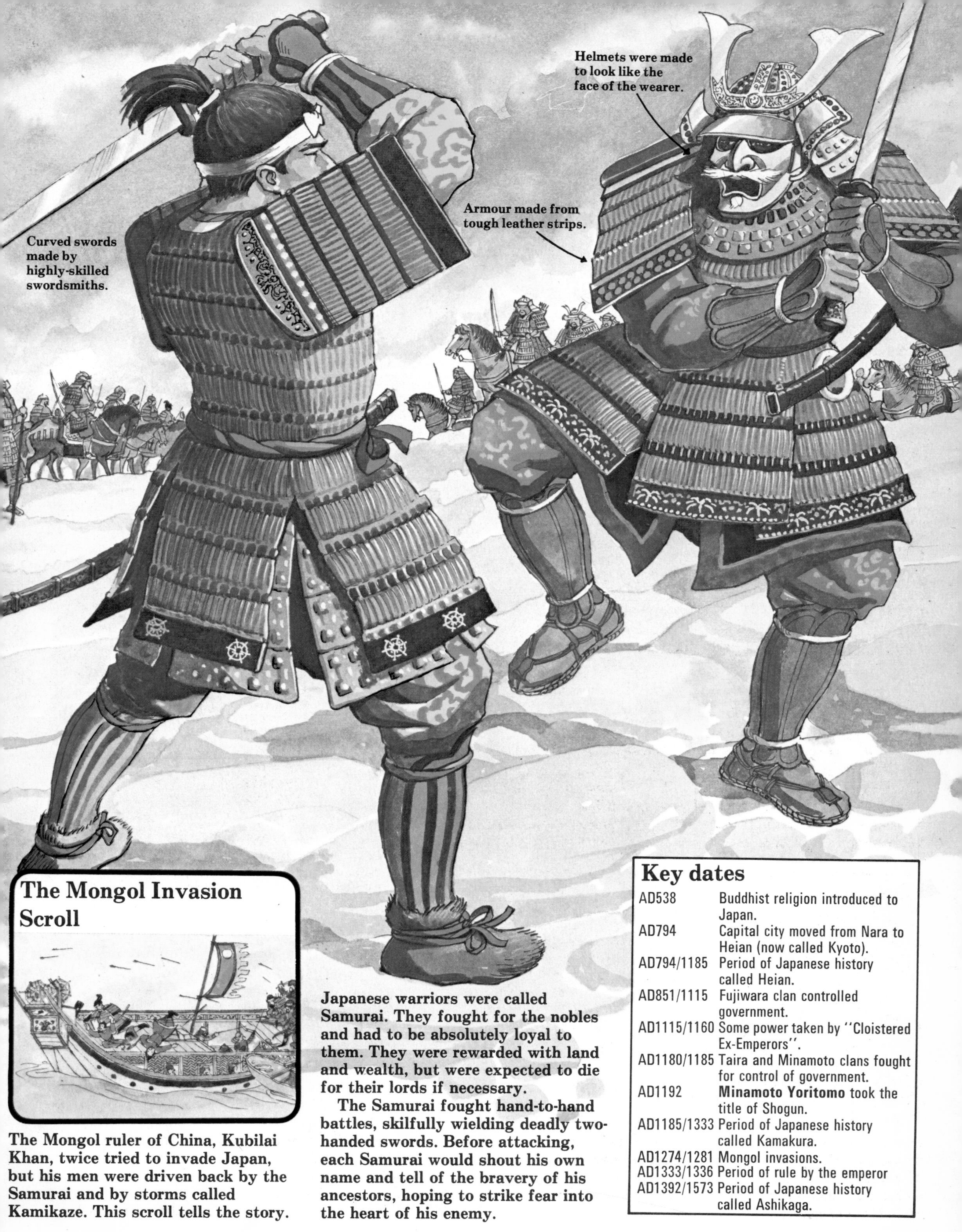


## The Mongol Invasion Scroll

The Mongol ruler of China, Kubilai Khan, twice tried to invade Japan, but his men were driven back by the Samurai and by storms called Kamikaze. This scroll tells the story.

Japanese warriors were called Samurai. They fought for the nobles and had to be absolutely loyal to them. They were rewarded with land and wealth, but were expected to die for their lords if necessary.

The Samurai fought hand-to-hand battles, skilfully wielding deadly two-handed swords. Before attacking, each Samurai would shout his own name and tell of the bravery of his ancestors, hoping to strike fear into the heart of his enemy.

## Key dates

| | |
|---|---|
| AD538 | Buddhist religion introduced to Japan. |
| AD794 | Capital city moved from Nara to Heian (now called Kyoto). |
| AD794/1185 | Period of Japanese history called Heian. |
| AD851/1115 | Fujiwara clan controlled government. |
| AD1115/1160 | Some power taken by ''Cloistered Ex-Emperors''. |
| AD1180/1185 | Taira and Minamoto clans fought for control of government. |
| AD1192 | **Minamoto Yoritomo** took the title of Shogun. |
| AD1185/1333 | Period of Japanese history called Kamakura. |
| AD1274/1281 | Mongol invasions. |
| AD1333/1336 | Period of rule by the emperor |
| AD1392/1573 | Period of Japanese history called Ashikaga. |

# Kingdoms, Traders and Tribes

In AD639, Arabs, inspired by their new religion, Islam, invaded Egypt and then north Africa. They traded with the local people and brought new wealth to the area.

South of the Sahara, the land was often difficult to clear and live in. There were also dangerous diseases there. As people learnt how to make strong tools from iron, tribes were able to progress further south, clearing and farming the land as they went.

## 1 West African kingdoms

Arab traders began to make regular journeys across the Sahara. They bought gold and salt from West Africa and sold it in busy Mediterranean ports.

## 2

Trade made the local Africans very rich. They built magnificent cities full of palaces and mosques. The most famous city was Timbuktu shown here.

## 3

Some of the West African rulers had large kingdoms. One of the most important was Mali. Several Arabs who travelled to these kingdoms kept records of their visits. They were very impressed by the luxury they found, especially at court. Here, some Arabs are meeting an African king.

## Portuguese explorers

From AD1420 onwards, Prince Henry of Portugal, known as "the Navigator", organized expeditions to explore the West African coast and trade with the Africans.

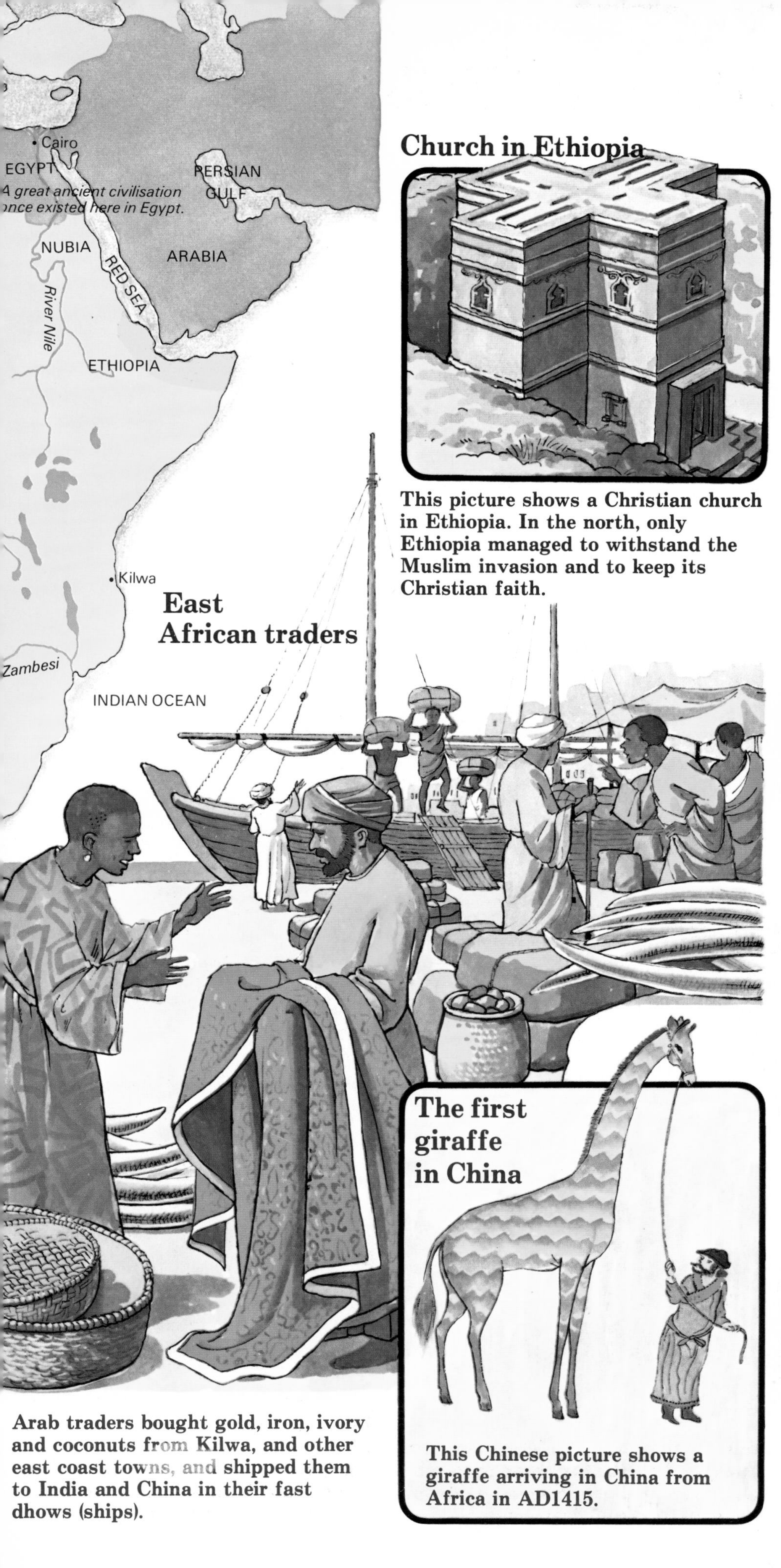


## Church in Ethiopia

This picture shows a Christian church in Ethiopia. In the north, only Ethiopia managed to withstand the Muslim invasion and to keep its Christian faith.

## East African traders

Arab traders bought gold, iron, ivory and coconuts from Kilwa, and other east coast towns, and shipped them to India and China in their fast dhows (ships).

## The first giraffe in China

This Chinese picture shows a giraffe arriving in China from Africa in AD1415.

## Life in the south

In the south different tribes adopted different ways of life.

In the Kalahari Desert the Bushmen hunted animals for their food.

Pygmies lived in tropical jungles, hunting animals and gathering berries and fruits.

Tribes living in the open plains of the east and south kept animals and farmed the land.

People who knew how to make iron tools were very useful to their tribes.

# Life in North and South America

At this time there were many separate groups of people living in different parts of the huge continent of America. In the forests, mountains, plains, deserts and jungles and in the frozen north, people found ways of surviving by hunting, fishing, gathering, and later farming. The people of North America did not have a system of writing, but archaeologists have found remains of their settlements, which tell us something about their lives.

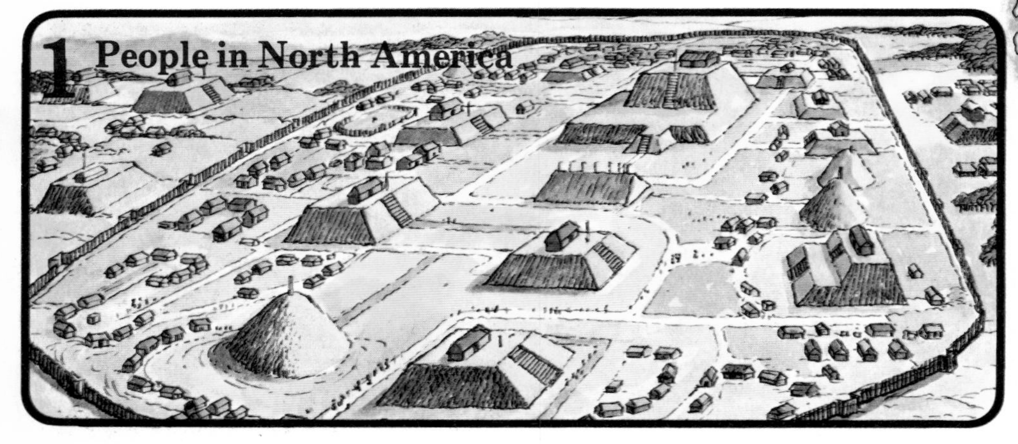

**1 People in North America**

**One of the most advanced groups of North American Indians were the Mississipians or "Mound Builders", who were farmers and traders. In their towns, the temples and other important buildings were built on top of great earth mounds. This picture shows part of Cahokia, one of their towns.**

**2**

**Underground rooms (kivas) were used for religious ceremonies.**

**Some Indian farmers lived in "pueblos", towns made of stone and mud. The houses were sometimes as high as five floors and were built in canyon walls.**

**3**

**At Huff, on the plains, traces of a village of more than 100 wooden houses, like this, have been found. The village was surrounded by a ditch and palisade (wooden fence).**

**4**

**Eskimos learnt how to live in the intense cold of the far north. They hunted caribou, seals and whales and also fished and trapped birds.**

## Mountain farmers in Peru

The first American farmers we know about lived in the area that is now Peru. They grew maize, vegetables, cotton, tobacco and a drug called coca. Later they built terraces on the mountainside, so that they could grow crops even on the steep slopes of the Andes. Alpacas and llamas provided wool and carried heavy loads.

## The Incas

These men are Inca warriors. The Incas were a tribe who lived in the mountains of Peru. The first Inca ruler probably lived about AD1200.

In 1438 a man called Pachacutec became their king and they spread out from the city of Cuzco, their capital, to conquer a huge empire.

## What the Indians made

The people in Peru were skilled potters and metal-workers and expert weavers. Some of the cloth they made has lasted to the present day and is still brightly-coloured. Each of the objects shown above was made by a different people.

## Towns

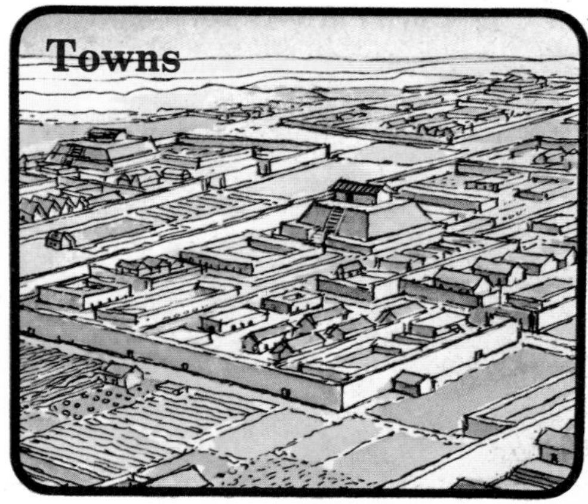

At first, the people of Peru had small settlements. Later they built great monuments and cities, such as the Chimu peoples' capital of Chanchan, shown above.

## Key dates

**North America**

| | |
|---|---|
| AD500/1500 | The Mound Builders or Mississipians lived. |
| AD1400/1600 | People living at Huff. |

**South America**

| | |
|---|---|
| AD200/900 | Period of Peruvian civilisation called the "Classic Period". |
| AD1100/1438 | Chimu people living at Chanchan. |
| AD1200 | **Manco Capac** ruled the Incas. |
| AD1438/1471 | **Pachacutec** ruled the Incas. |

**Central America**

| | |
|---|---|
| 700BC/AD900 | Maya living in Yucatan. |
| 100BC | Zapotecs living on the south coast. |
| AD750/990 | The Toltec Empire. |
| AD1325 | Aztecs known to be at Tenochtitlan. |

# The Aztecs

One of the earliest and greatest peoples of Central America were the Maya. This picture shows a procession of Mayan musicians.

Archaeologists have recently discovered, in the same area, more about a people called the Toltecs. This is a temple in Tula, their capital city.

This is an Aztec warrior. The Aztecs probably came from western Mexico before they settled at Tenochtitlan and conquered all the land around it.

The Aztecs had a system of numbers, which meant they could count and keep records of their possessions. These are some of the symbols they used.

This picture shows the "New Fire Ceremony", which marked the beginning of a 52 year cycle. There were 18 months in each year.

## The market place

Trading between themselves and with people from other towns was an important part of Aztec life. They had no money so they exchanged goods for others of equal value. This is called barter. Chocolate was a favourite drink, so cocoa beans, from which it was made, were always in demand. They were often used for making small payments. Jade and turquoise were more valuable than gold and silver.

Children were taught by their parents. At 15 the boys went to school. Special schools trained boys and girls as priests.

## The city of Tenochtitlan

This is the capital city of the Aztecs. It was built on islands in the middle of a lake. The lake no longer exists and modern Mexico City is built on top of it.

The Aztecs worshipped many gods and goddesses. They built temples where they killed human beings and ripped out their hearts, in order to please these gods.

### Mosaic and feathers

Aztec craftsmen produced beautiful mosaic work, like this mask, which is covered with small pieces of precious turquoise.

Shields, like this one, were made of feathers. The Aztecs also used feathers for making head-dresses and cloaks.

### How we know

The Aztecs used a form of picture-writing. It had not developed far enough to record complicated ideas but some religious teachings and history were recorded and have survived in books like the one above. Such a book is called a codex.

# Index



# Going Further

## Books to read

These are some of the books available on this period of history. If you look in your local library or bookshop, you will probably find lots of others.

*The Time Traveller Book of Viking Raiders* by Anne Civardi and James Graham-Campbell (Usborne).
*The Time Traveller Book of Knights and Castles* by Judy Hindley (Usborne).
*Castle* by David Macaulay (Collins).
*Living in a Medieval Village, Living in a Medieval City* and *Living in a Crusader Land*—3 books by R. J. Unstead (Black).
**Knight Crusader* by Ronald Welch (Puffin).
**The Children's Crusade* by Henry Treece (Puffin).
**Vinland the Good* by Henry Treece (Puffin).
*The Discovery of the World Vol 1: Conquerors and Invaders* by Bernard Planche (Moonlight Publishing).
*Factbook of History* (Galley Press).
*The Samurai of Japan* and *Genghis Khan and the Mongols*—2 books by Michael Gibson (Wayland).
*Peoples of the Past, The Aztecs* by Judith Crosher (Macdonald).

**These books are novels.*

## Places to visit

If you live in Britain, two books that will help you find out about places to visit in your area are *Museums and Galleries in Great Britain and Ireland* and *Historic Houses, Castles and Gardens in Great Britain and Ireland* (British Leisure Publications). Both these books are published every year.

In London the British Museum, the Victoria and Albert Museum and the London Museum all have collections of things from this period of history.

In Australia the National Gallery of Victoria in Melbourne has a good collection of objects from Cambodia, China and Japan. It is also worth visiting the museums in Perth and Sydney.

In Canada the best museums to visit are the Royal Ontario Museum in Toronto and the McCord Museum in Montreal.